DENTISTS

by Charly Haley

Cody Koala

An Imprint of Pop!

popbooksonline.com

abdopublishing.com

Published by Pop!, a division of ABDO, PO Box 398166, Minneapolis, Minnesota 55439. Copyright © 2019 by POP, LLC. International copyrights reserved in all countries. No part of this book may be reproduced in any form without written permission from the publisher. Pop!™ is a trademark and logo of POP, LLC.

Printed in the United States of America, North Mankato, Minnesota

042018
092018

 THIS BOOK CONTAINS RECYCLED MATERIALS

Distributed in paperback by North Star Editions, Inc.

Cover Photo: iStockphoto
Interior Photos: iStockphoto, 1, 21; Shutterstock Images, 5 (top), 5 (bottom left), 5 (bottom right) 6, 7, 9, 11, 12, 15, 16, 19 (top left), 19 (top right), 19 (bottom)

Editor: Meg Gaertner
Series Designer: Laura Mitchell

Library of Congress Control Number: 2017963075
Publisher's Cataloging-in-Publication Data
Names: Haley, Charly, author.
Title: Dentists / by Charly Haley.
Description: Minneapolis, Minnesota : Pop!, 2019. | Series: Community workers | Includes online resources and index.
Identifiers: ISBN 9781532160097 (lib.bdg.) | ISBN 9781635178043 (pbk) | ISBN 9781532161216 (ebook).
Subjects: LCSH: Dentists--Juvenile literature. | Teeth--Care and hygiene--Juvenile literature. | Dentistry--Juvenile literature. | Occupations--Careers--Jobs--Juvenile literature. | Community life—Juvenile literature.
Classification: DDC 617.6--dc23

Hello! My name is

Cody Koala

Pop open this book and you'll find QR codes like this one, loaded with information, so you can learn even more!

Scan this code* and others like it while you read, or visit the website below to make this book pop.

popbooksonline.com/dentists

*Scanning QR codes requires a web-enabled smart device with a QR code reader app and a camera.

Table of Contents

Chapter 1

A Day in the Life

Dentists look inside their **patients'** mouths. They look to see if their patients' teeth and **gums** are healthy.

Dentists will give patients **floss**, a toothbrush, and toothpaste to take home.

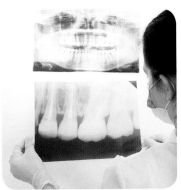

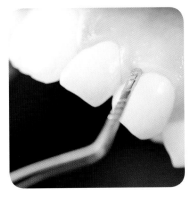

Watch a video here!

Dentists tell people
about the best ways to
floss and brush their teeth.

People's teeth and gums will stay healthy if they do as their dentists say.

Chapter 2

The Work

Dentists have helpers
who clean patients' teeth.
These helpers also aid
dentists in seeing if patients'
teeth and gums are healthy.

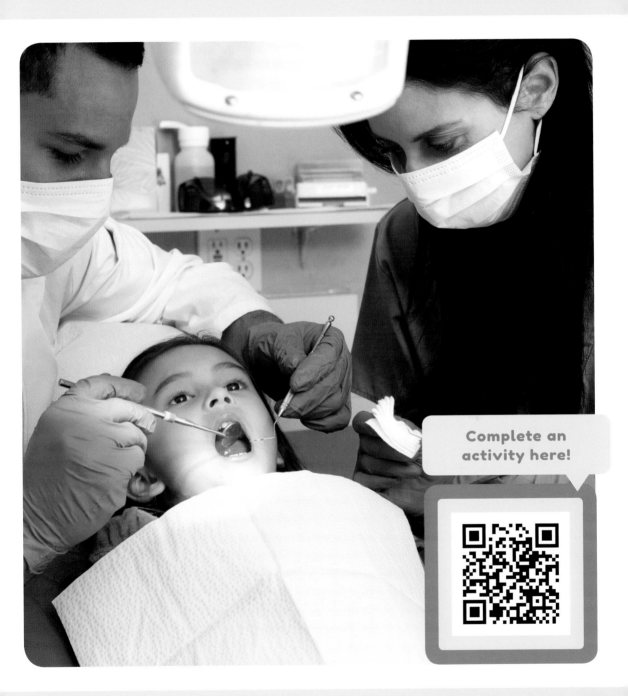

Complete an activity here!

Sometimes people get small holes in their teeth called **cavities**. The dentist will put a **filling** in the cavity to fix it.

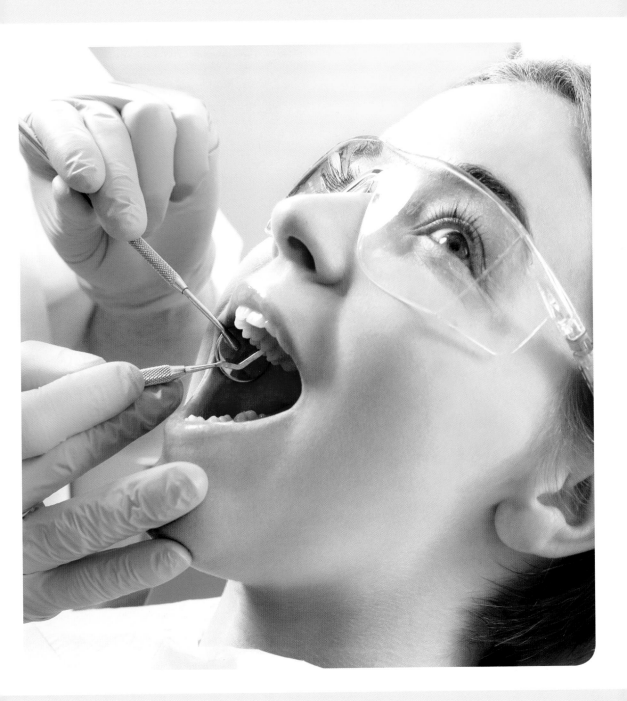

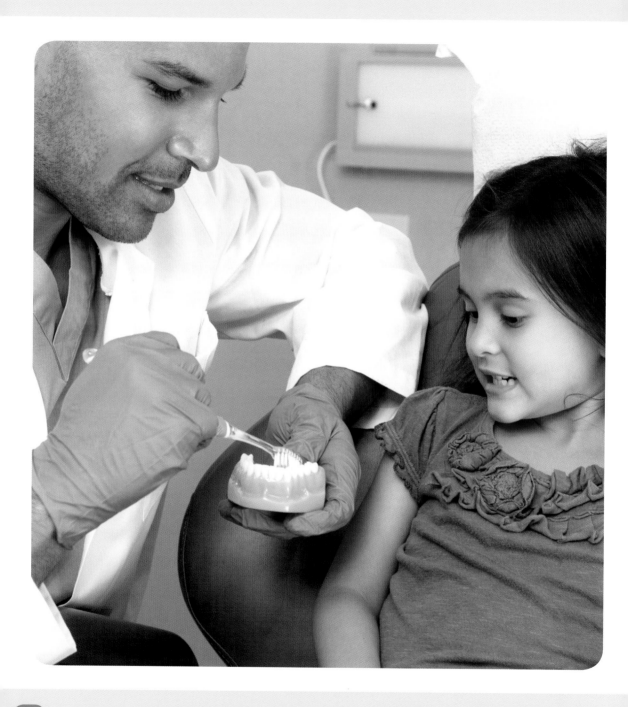

Dentists teach people how to keep their teeth healthy. They teach people that eating the wrong foods can cause cavities.

Chapter 3

Tools for Dentists

Patients sit in a chair that leans back so dentists can look into their mouths. Dentists shine a light to help them see in patients' mouths.

Learn more here!

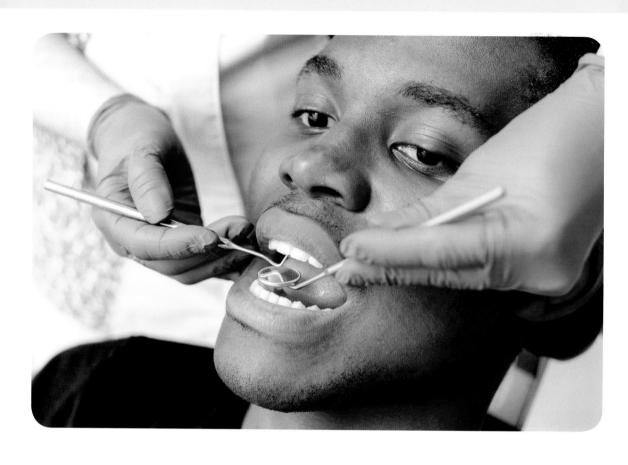

Dentists hold a small
mirror so they can see all
sides of a patient's teeth.

Dentists use different metal tools to check teeth and poke gums to see if they are healthy.

Dentists use an X-ray machine to take pictures of patients' teeth. If they find a problem, dentists might use a drill. The drill can help dentists fill cavities.

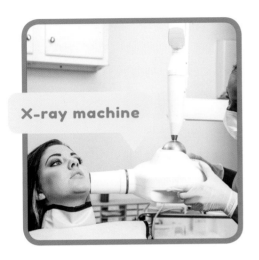

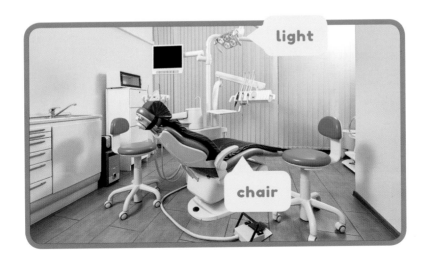

Chapter 4

Helping the Community

It hurts people to have unhealthy teeth. Dentists help people keep their teeth healthy. They help people have beautiful, clean smiles.

In some places in the world, it's hard for people to find a dentist to help them.

Learn more here!

Making Connections

Text-to-Self

Have you been to the dentist? What did you think of your visit?

Text-to-Text

Have you read other books about community workers? How are their jobs similar to or different from a dentist's?

Text-to-World

In some places in the world, people can't go to the dentist. Why do you think it's important that we have dentists?

Glossary

cavity – a small hole in a tooth created when the tooth is decaying, or dying.

filling – something used to fill a cavity in a tooth.

floss – a thin thread used to clean between the teeth.

gums – the pink area in a person's mouth that holds teeth in place.

patient – someone who goes to a doctor or dentist in need of care.

Index

Online Resources

popbooksonline.com

Thanks for reading this Cody Koala book!

Scan this code* and others like it in this book, or visit the website below to make this book pop!

popbooksonline.com/dentists

*Scanning QR codes requires a web-enabled smart device with a QR code reader app and a camera.